1956

a collection of short stories
by
Margaret Wilkinson

Guest Editor Gerry Wardle

*First published November 2000
reprinted March 2003 by:
Diamond Twig
5 Bentinck Road
Newcastle upon Tyne
NE4 6UT
Tel: (0191) 273 5326
Fax: (0191) 273 5326
Email: diamond.twig@virgin.net
Website: www.diamondtwig.co.uk*

Typeset in Palatino 10/12pt

Printed by Peterson Printers, South Shields

© Margaret Wilkinson

ISBN 0 9539196 0 9

*Diamond Twig acknowledges the
financial assistance of Northern Arts*

For Frieda Platt

Contents

5   Why I write
7   Lingerie
20   1956
30   The Mapmaker
39   The Moon
49   Little Bird
57   Gertie and Moe
60   Where Is The Air Coming In ?
70   Dowsing In The North East Of England

The reason I write is explained in the following memoir.
My aunt Frieda and I sat in a white foreign car called a Renault Dauphin. It was the kind of car my father never would have owned. Although it was not a sports car, it had a slanted outline and was dangerously low to the ground. Frieda was waiting until six pm when she could leave her vehicle on Eighth Avenue without risking a parking ticket from the City of New York.

She didn't have much time left. It was spring. In the autumn, my aunt would be leaving me. She didn't die on a wet country road, but on a brief holiday after a lingering illness. No one had told me she was ill.

That evening, she was making notes for a short story she was writing in a dainty, white, plastic-covered book decorated with fleur-de-lis. I say plastic, but in those days nothing looked artificial. Plastic was beautiful. Frieda's cramped handwriting, words overwritten, crossed out, trailing along the sides of the page, blossomed. I wondered why she was writing so fervently, and how she would ever read it again. She might have been using flower language for all I knew. The pages of this book were far too small. Then and there, I noticed how much suffering and joy writing caused.

Frieda didn't even lift her head, but I was startled when, on the other side of Eighth Avenue, *The Egyptian Gardens*, a Middle Eastern nightclub featuring bellydancers, switched on a band of jellied neon lights. I moved my stomach experimentally. (On the east side of town, it was rumoured, dancing girls shimmied topless in cages.) Secretly I was interested in all that blowsy, redhot stuff. If I started immediately, I could transform myself. I'd been a melancholy child. My hair was parted and brushed over one side of my brow. I had more imagination than looks. Aunt Frieda was wearing a black jacket. Soon I would lose her. She smoked a Pall Mall like it was a Gauloise, in the corner of her mouth. I lacked her cool, but I wanted to be her. 'Is writing fun?' I asked. In those days, my voice was a sweet tremolo. My head turned upwards to gaze at her.

'It's a hellava stinking life,' she said. She spoke through her nose, like everyone else in New York.

After that, I remember sitting quietly. A kind of shocked slackness I'd never now tolerate surrounded Frieda and I. Scrolls of neon shivered in the arched corners of the eyeglasses she wore. Her pen writhed passionately across the page. At once I realised there was a choice to be made. I considered my options as if they were twin candles. I was thirteen years old, still waiting for life to begin. Nervously, I wondered how quickly I could learn to shimmy. It was either shimmy or write. I lifted my eyebrows and pursed my lips like a valentine.

Lingerie

I needed some new clothes pronto. That dress was it. A black sheath with a large flat bow on the backside. I'd seen it in the department store where I worked and had to have it. My saliva dried up with determination. I wanted something that would make me look good. That dress. Maybe gloves.

My small shapely feet were made for ballroom dancing. I was round and sleek with dark, glossy hair, blood red nails. Not too tall. Once upon a time, men chased after me. These days, let's face it, the air was thinning. I had to advertise. I was waiting for a man with wraparound sunglasses, like a celebrity. I didn't have forever. The clothes in my wardrobe were already starting to droop. My underwear was gone - held up by safety pins. I had to take control of my life. Turn things around. Think positive. Get back on track. Put myself on display. Find someone to replace that dickhead Ernie. How was I supposed to know he was married? I wasn't a homewrecker. After today, he was like poison to me. Guys had been trying to kill me for years. First I thought Ernie, a snazzy dresser himself, would buy me the cocktail gown I'd been eyeing. But I didn't want nothing from a married man. I'd rather ask Flo. Flo and I worked together in the Lingerie Department at MACY'S 34th Street. She was marking an order book at the counter when I got in. I'd never asked her for a loan before. But I thought, what the heck? I was early. I had fifteen minutes left on my lunch hour. The floor was dead. I could have read *Confidential* in the stock room, mooning over Bill Holden and Burt Lancaster. In my handbag I had *Peyton Place*. It was the juiciest novel of 1956. I could have read some of that. I could have let my long hair down in the employees' restroom and tried out some new styles. But I joined Flo at the counter. She was an older woman with a grey face, really tired clothes and a flat hairdo. She was a MACY'S GIRL, which meant she'd been with the firm for twenty years.

In front of management, I addressed her formally. She was Miss Hirschorn. I was Marguerite. Today she was wearing a prim white blouse, her MACY'S GIRL badge pinned to her collar and a nothing skirt. Perhaps it was the loose shoes that gave her away. I looked a little closer. She had dry lines around her mouth.

'Busy?'

Flo shook her head. She had no personality.

'Anything I can do?' I tried to butter her up. She opened her small eyes wide. 'You feeling all right?' She looked at me suspiciously. 'Why don't you check the floor stock?'

I walked to the cabinet where the conservative half slips, full slips and underpants, with different length legs from long to extra long in a range of sizes, were kept. Flo gave me a tight smile as I pulled out the top drawer and bent my head over it. When she went behind the stacks to eat her sandwich, I got busy. I made a list of all the sizes, colours and styles we needed to replenish. Then I followed her into the stockroom. Flo jumped when she saw me and swiped her lips with the back of her hand. 'Are you leaving the floor unattended?' she asked icily.

I tried and failed to imagine Flo in a happy place like a cocktail lounge. Abandoning the stock, I returned to the floor. There were no customers to serve, so I looked around for something else I could do. Using the key we kept in the cash register I opened a drawer and admired the lacy half-bras. There were some big boxes stacked on top of a cabinet with sliding glass doors that stood behind our counter. Flo didn't want to unpack these boxes. She'd said her arms hurt. But I knew better. They were full of French shorties. She didn't like that frothy stuff. She'd told me she'd put in for a transfer to Luggage. But management wanted her on Lingerie - with her experience.

Stiffly I climbed the step ladder we used, reached up with both hands, rummaged around and started to lift down the top box. I had the big box almost in my hands when I heard a snap and sensed a slithering under my blouse, as both shoulder straps on the old slip I was wearing tore loose. The safety pins must have let go. That's how badly I needed new clothes, underwear included. I came down the ladder. For no good reason, I laughed. Men said I had a theatrical air. I looked over my shoulder. The Lingerie Department was empty. Lucky me. I stepped out of the worn pink satinette. It felt smooth and wet in my hands. No one saw as I mashed the slip into my shoulderbag, which was kept under the counter.

Flo came back from lunch, staggering only a bit, and picked up the order book again. 'Have you been touching this?' she asked, raising her unplucked eyebrows. I shook my head. She frowned and looked through the pages. She had a sour stomach and was sucking a Tums. She looked very tense standing the way she did with her straight thin back and her rigid neck. In a few years I could end up like her. That's why I needed the dress. Maybe even shoes.

'Flo,' I came right out with it. 'I'm a bit short this month. Have you got anything spare?'

We didn't know each other very well, despite the fact we'd worked together a long time. Optimistically, I imagined us touching highball glasses in a nightclub. 'I don't need much.' Nervously, I squeezed a pile of neatly folded panties on the counter-top. Then I looked up and gave her my most radiant smile.

A parched look from Flo. 'I'm afraid not.' She sucked her dry cheeks.

'I'll pay you right back,' I promised.

Flo got MACY'S GIRLS' enhanced salary. She made enough to give me a loan. 'I like you Marguerite,' she said brusquely, looking everywhere but at me. 'But no, it's impossible.' She picked up her pencil. 'It isn't anything serious?' she whispered.

'Anything medical?' she asked with enthusiasm.

'There's a dress I want,' I blurted out. 'Beyond my price range, even with an employee discount. But oh. You should see it.' The remembered smell of a new dress made my heart lurch.

'You want to buy a dress?'

When I nodded, I could feel the skin around my mouth wobble. 'I have to catch a man. I want a turban too.'

'A turban would suit you.' She poked her terrible hair. If she was shocked, she didn't show it. She put her pencil behind her ear.

'And long gloves,' I added. 'And...'

'Let me give you a piece of advice Marguerite,' she cut me off. 'Save your money.' She glanced over her shoulder to make sure no one was around to listen. 'You ought to be more like me. Every month I put something aside. When you don't have a husband, you have to take care of yourself.' She took hold of my sleeve. 'Because there's going to be trouble. There's always trouble. Trouble with neighbours, for instance.'

I found what she was saying shocking and glared at her. Didn't she think I was going to get a husband? She patted me on the shoulder, then turned away like the subject was closed.

'Are you going to lend me the money? Or not?'

She shook her head. 'Why don't you apply to be a MACY'S GIRL? You've been here long enough.' She hunched her thin neck and began to busy herself with her orders again.

I edged away from her. What did she mean? This job was nothing to me. I was only marking time till something better came along. 'Okay,' I said. 'I'll think about it.' I balled my hands in my pockets. It wasn't the money. The money didn't really matter. There was more to it than that. There was her tone of voice, her shitty advice, her idea that we were in the same boat. No way was I like her. I wasn't as young as I used to be, no longer a slip of a girl, I was willing to understand that, but the rest of it? 'Hey,' I shouted. 'You and me, we're not alike.' Flo was wrinkled and nothing out of the ordinary - except in one respect. 'You're an old bag and an old souse!' I shouted. I felt sluttish without a slip. My skirt caught between my legs.

She didn't respond. But stiffly, like she was made out of a block of wood, she lowered her head until it was almost resting on her order book. I stood with my hands splayed now on the counter, glaring at her. I wouldn't drop my eyes. No way would I drop my eyes. Then I pressed my elbows to my sides, concealing the place where my inner arms had gone crepey. Suddenly I felt tired and alone. Without a new dress how was I going to put myself back on display? A happy life was slipping from my grasp. Flo was a stuck-up, dried-up twig. And Ernie? He was a louse.

Ernie was all elbows, ribs and knees. He was going to be my ticket out of MACY'S. Then at lunch today, it came to me - he's married. I don't know how

I'd missed the signs before. The way he kept twitching his shoulders and turning around. Looking around. Then looking back at me. There was someone in that restaurant he didn't want to meet. 'I'm not hungry,' he said when the food came. 'Let's get out of here.'

I knew it anyway. I was just kidding myself. For one thing, he'd only given me his work number. 'Don't you have a home phone?' I asked. 'I work a lot,' he said. 'You can always reach me there.' Oh yeah. Him and his leather business. While I was punching the clock at MACY'S, he was wholesale-ing calfskin purses uptown. I thought, leather, he's probably a rich guy. But he was a cheapskate. If he had money, he didn't spend it on me. I thought about the dark, empty places he took me. I expected nightclub society in the afternoon. Sardi's, Birdland. How long did I have to wait? Today we ate in a dive on 38th street. Dark? Of course it was dark. I don't know who he thought he saw there. Some neighbour? A friend of his wife's?

So why would I want this tragedy? I didn't like him anyway. He was skinny. I like a nice, big guy. This guy was wiry. Even his hair was skinny. At one time I actually considered a love pregnancy with him. I must have had a screw loose.

After he paid the bill, Ernie escorted me into the street, a big guilty sign around his neck. I'd rather eat at the Automat, I was thinking. I'd rather eat a meatball hero in a pizzeria. Often I did. I had a steel-lined stomach like a guy.

The bright afternoon sunlight put ten years on me. Away from the restaurant, Ernie led me into a quiet doorway. 'Do you still love me?' he asked. He was no dope. He knew what I was thinking. But I wouldn't even look him in the eye. Then he took out his wallet and tried to give me ten dollars. 'I'm sorry,' he said.

'Forget it,' I told him. 'I don't want your money.' I shoved his hand away. I had my principles. 'I don't go with married men.'

He tried to tell me how his wife, Selma, didn't understand him. Honestly! I cringed. 'In the restaurant you were ashamed to be seen with me. I'm not having that.'

When we said goodbye, he ran his hands up and down my back and tried to cover me with himself. I could feel his heart beat against mine. He asked me to give him time. Then he soothed my back some more. I have to admit, it felt nice. They all do it - make you feel nice, for a minute. He didn't look too lousy. His face was in-love, as if I really meant something to him. His lips, as he was about to kiss me, opened. I couldn't help myself. Temporarily, he was like the stars to me.

I was soft on men. I let Ernie put his tongue in my ear. But he was a clunker. I wasn't packing a torch for him. I walked very firmly away.

I unboxed a lime-green short nightdress with a low neckline and spaghetti straps. I draped it over a display table, with an I-couldn't-care-less attitude. When I looked up, I saw Flo staring like she felt sorry for me. Like it was me who'd been drinking on the job. I glared back. This was war. I picked up the sexy nightdress and jiggled it in front of her. She dropped her eyes and moved off towards a rack of flannel pyjamas. I watched her with contempt and wondered if she'd noticed how big her behind was getting. She was thin on top with a big bottom. She needed a girdle with two-way stretch. Just then, the elevator door opened and a man came out.

'Hello Willard.' Flo waved a couple of fingers at the security guard, as if everything was normal on Lingerie. As if there wasn't an atmosphere between us.

'Miss Hirschorn.' He nodded to her, but didn't say anything to me. 'Can't stop to talk.' He was heading towards the central stock room where he broke down cardboard boxes in the afternoons. I couldn't help but notice the white socks he wore, like gym socks, with his polished, black leather shoes.

Willard, the uniformed security guard, asked me out on a date once. He put the moves on me, but I turned him down flat. I wasn't going out with him. No way. He watched the floor for shoplifters, staff as well as customers. He took his stupid job seriously and looked like a jerk. He probably made a buck twenty an hour.

After I rejected him, Willard stopped being nice. He walked past in his nerdy shoes, as if I wasn't there.

I was too wrapped up in sorting out the foundation garments to even notice. Busily, I dressed a wooden torso we used for display purposes in a fine, but modest, satin all-in-one with concealed stitching. Soon the customers started coming in. There were plenty. Enough so that the cash register opened and closed often.

I couldn't wait to belt off work. I should have just left with a headache. If I stayed, I was going to do something dangerous that afternoon. I didn't know what exactly. No, that wasn't true. I knew. I began watching my hands. Probably I wasn't thinking clearly. The metal drawer was divided into neat cubby holes. While I was making change from a sale, I just reached in. I took twenty dollars. Then I took twenty again. I shut my eyes. I didn't even want to see what I was doing.

When I opened my eyes, I saw wormy blue veins on the backs of my hands. No wedding ring. Age spots. Another twenty slid up into my palm. At the very least, I'd probably lose my job. But I was hot under the collar. Having to ask Flo. For what? For nothing. And Ernie? I fumed at the thought of all the time I'd wasted on Ernie.

Three swipes and I closed the drawer with a loud slam. Turning around, I pretended to look for something inside the lingerie cabinet. Shocked, I saw a lizard-skin face, like my mother's, glaring at me from the sliding glass doors.

I was afraid to leave the store that night. Moving as if in a dream, I knew I was probably never coming back. I was already regretting my actions. Staff never took money. It was too easy to trace. In the employees' restroom mirror my face looked small and frightened, old and loose. The lines that ran from my nose to my mouth were vivid. I washed my hands in the sink. My makeup was dead white. Sighing, I smoothed away the little creases on my forehead. Tonight I'd put fresh sheets on the fold-out bed in my rented room. Then I'd fry a pork chop on my hot plate and have a bath. I owned a radio, an electric fan and an iron. Resting up, I'd listen to *'Stop the Music'* and *'The Steve Allen Show.'* I slipped a bar of employees' soap in my pocket. Usually I went out in the evening. But I had nothing left to wear, there was no one in the city who loved me and I had no life in this world anymore.

Willard was standing at his customary place by the door, eyeballing the exiting staff. Especially the women. No one was excused. I held my shoulderbag close to my body. 'You,' he said, hovering between me and the door. 'Step over here.' He had a little table where he examined things. 'Open up,' he said. I put my bag on the table. A piece of pink satin material peeked out the top. You had to have x-ray eyes to see it. 'What's this?' he asked in a loud voice. He had a flashlight attached to his belt and a screwdriver. He moved closer. Suddenly I was the nervous, silent type.

My hands were shaking so much I couldn't undo the clasp. He undid it for me. Then he put his big paw inside. 'Aaahhhaa.' He pulled out my busted slip, broken straps dangling. Behind me, waiting employees buzzed impatiently, giving me slimy looks. I was so humiliated, I thought I was going to faint. Willard looked shocked himself. One corner of his mouth jerked up and down. He blinked and kept staring. I guess he believed he was going to catch me with stolen goods. But he recovered. Holding up my torn lingerie must have been the next best thing. When he saw *Peyton Place* inside my shoulderbag, he chuckled and shook one finger back and forth at me. I just bent my head. I wished I could do this afternoon over again. Without looking up, I took back my things. Willard opened the security lock and released the bolt.

Even then, my optimistic nature surfaced and I dared to imagine Ernie on his knees telling me he was going to leave his wife for me. Or better yet, telling me he wasn't really married, that he'd only said he was married to test me - and asking me to marry him right away, then bending over to kiss the hem of the dress I was going to buy.

The air was soft and warm. It was summer and the sky was still light. It must have rained because the pavement was wet, smelling clean and brackish at the same time. For a moment, forgetting Ernie, I leaned against the staff exit, covered my eyes and listened to the sounds of the outside world. Then I left, with a lousy sixty dollars crumpled in my shoe.

1956

I decided to kill my brother-in-law after dinner. When he was stuffed and sluggish, I'd ask him up to the roof for a smoke. It was Labour Day weekend. I'd say he fell. It was broiling hot. The roof was a good place. People went up in hot weather. It wouldn't look suspicious.

I did worry about the neighbours. For a moment, I felt nervous. But I calmed down. If anyone joined us up there, I'd think of something else to do to Arthur. I sat with my hands bunched up in my pockets, clenching and unclenching my fists, imagining all the other ways I could kill him. Terrible troubles hung over me.

Every Sunday my wife and I went from our apartment in Queens to Flatbush in Brooklyn to eat with her parents, Gertrude and Moe, and her older brother, Arthur. Arthur was a bachelor who lived alone in the Bronx. Even in this heat, he wore a three piece suit and a dark tie. With an oddball groan, he sat down in an armchair opposite me. He had plump hands, unsteady cheeks and a big soft frame. Carefully, he crossed one leg over the other. I resolved to tear out his throat.

The Flatbush sky had been overcast all morning. It was airless and humid. From my in-laws' living room window, sunlight glowered behind the clouds. If it rained, Arthur and I certainly couldn't go up to the roof. Never mind, I'd silence him somehow. I tried to decide between rodent poison and piano wire. My wife's family had coarsened me. If it came to a fight, I wasn't sure who would win. I was thin and wiry with an undernourished chest and bushy, black hair, slicked down with Brylcreem. Arthur was bulkier.

Across the room, the TV glinted in a wooden cabinet. Looking at it, I could feel sweat hanging from my armpits. An old fan was turning ineffectually on a shelf. I almost retched. 'What's for dinner?' I asked my mother-in-law. Like I had to ask. The smell of roast chicken poured out of the kitchen door, along with the smell of boiling harnesses, which meant my mother-in-law's cabbage soup. My stomach twisted into a foamy knot. I sat on the edge of my seat. I would have liked to take my shirt off, put my hands behind my head, lay back and let my legs dangle over the arm of the couch. But Gertrude, my mother-in-law, would have had kittens. I hated her phoney airs. In frustration, I rabbit-punched a throw pillow. Everyone else sat around giving each other dainty looks. What a sick bunch! I glared at them. Arthur in particular. I imagined myself chasing him down Courtelyou Road.

Arthur was an accountant for a Greenpoint slaughterhouse, a brewery on Bushwick Avenue and a few restaurants in Manhattan. (My father-in-law, Arthur's father, ate Manhattan restaurants for dinner and spat them out. He was shrewd and crooked when he was in his prime.)

Arthur leaned forward and offered me a cigarette. Like I would take a cigarette from him? No way would I do that. I resented his earnest face. When he proffered his open pack of mentholated Kools, I had to gaze down at my shoes. While my eyes washed the carpet, I made up my mind to knife him in the kidneys.

'How can you call Adlai Stevenson a contender?' my wife Selma was saying in her high, whining voice. Arthur smiled uneasily. They all knew I was a registered Democrat. 'Eisenhower's a contender. But Stevenson's a egghead and nothing else.' Selma tried to pick a fight.

'Oh go to hell,' I told her, causing the heat to move around in my mouth. I purposely stared over her head at a rubber plant. It smouldered in the hazy sunlight. On the wall behind it hung our wedding photograph. Selma wore a kitten dress and veil. I stood beside her in this photo like a pale dog, my dark hair hidden under a top hat.

'Don't be fresh,' Selma scolded. She blinked her eyes a couple of times and pressed her lips together. At home she made too many phone calls, carelessly wasting money.

'Stevenson is Stevenson, and Eisenhower is Eisenhower,' my father-in-law, the gangster-peacemaker, put in.

'Eisenhower?' my mother-in-law doddered. 'Is that a Jewish name?'

'How's business?' Arthur asked me, innocent,

guileless. Without answering, I got up and walked restlessly over to the window. Selma's brother sickened and frightened me. I could smell dog shit on his shoes. For an instant, I rested my head on the window glass. 'What are you doing Ernie?' my wife complained.

Selma inherited her father's head for crooked business. She used to sell individual retirement funds to the self-employed. She took kickbacks, and concessions. She was a sharpie. She sniffed around. She learned from her father. But she quit work when we got married. 'Married women don't work,' her mother told her. At home all day, Selma seethed. 'You think you're in business?' she'd taunted me. 'I don't call what you do business.' I shrank away from her.

Her mother, old eagle eyes, knew something was wrong. She studied me anxiously. I could feel her sharp gaze behind my back. The view from the window was of an airshaft full of neatly lidded garbage pails. I looked out listlessly. The pails shimmered in the heat. Then I saw the building's superintendent wandering around in his spotless overalls, making sure all the lids were on tight. This place is a grave, I thought. They're gonna bury me if I don't get out quick. Arthur was the one holding the shovel. He winked elaborately in my direction. Selma's jowly brother was more successful in business than me. I hated his bulging cheeks.

When I married Selma, my father-in-law set me

up in leather goods. By now I owed him plenty. In the beginning I borrowed his money without compunction. But I made some bad investments. I wasn't a commercial person. I used to drive a cab. At present, everything I owned was tied up in skins. Summer was my slow period. Nobody wanted leather at this time of year. I couldn't even move a purse. Only recently did I realise the hole I'd dug myself into. I should have stayed a cab driver. Any minute my father-in-law, Moe, might call in his loans. He had some nasty friends in the Jewish Mafia. Every time we visited, he'd ask Selma if I was treating her right. Not even trying to conceal the sneer in his voice, he'd glare at me contemptuously. Moe Goldfarb was still handsome in a decrepit way. He wore good suits and had his nails buffed. In his youth he'd been violent in Rockaway Beach. He washed money in Woodlawn. Burglary was a side-dish.

His son Arthur crossed his legs prissily at his ankles. He wore a cheap, plastic belt. He must have thought no one would notice a belt from Taiwan. I noticed. It was an insult. Belts were my business. Why didn't he come to me? I'd have given him a rock bottom price on a real leather, American belt with a hidden money pouch.

By now the armpits of my sports shirt were soaking. I could feel the sweat dribble down my sides, as Arthur uncrossed his ankles, then re-crossed them again. I'd never killed a man before.

'Do the business,' I told myself.

The air was numbed with the smell of chicken. At a glance from my father-in-law, my wife and her mother jumped up and began setting the large dining table that stood in one corner of the living room. My father-in-law studied his gold watch. '2:30,' he said, which meant it was time to eat. He was a jerk, but I admired him. I owed him up to the roof. It was Arthur I hated. Arthur was a rodent. I thought about surprising him in a dark alley with a baseball bat.

When we sat down to eat there was a dispute about the fan. 'You want to move the fan?' my mother-in-law asked, but her question was more like an order than an inquiry.

'Nah,' my father-in-law said, knotting his hands.

'It's blowing in the wrong direction.'

'I'm not getting up Gertrude.'

She looked miserable. 'So let it stay,' she said to Arthur in an aggrieved voice.

Immediately Arthur jumped to his feet and picked up the fan. He tried to pull it to the table where we were sitting, without unplugging it. Jerked, the frayed cord sputtered, leaving a trail of black smoke. What a dope! I tightened my grip on his murder. How could I trust a dope like Arthur?

A small flame crackled along the wiring. Arthur stepped on it with his mincing feet. I glared at him. Would he say anything? I couldn't be sure. Arthur's lid was on tight. But was it tight enough? I'd have to kill him soon. I thought of electrocuting him, like the government electrocuted the Rosenbergs. But for the moment, I was laying low. I drank a sip of water.

'Forget it.' Selma's father chewed with his mouth open. 'I'm gonna call a repairman.'

For that piece of junk? I thought. I couldn't wait for leather-weather. I decided to kill Arthur with a blow to the back of his head.

'Where you going to get an electrician on a Sunday? I queried brightly, careful not to sneer at my father-in-law.

'But Ernie,' my wife leaned towards me, 'the electrician probably owes daddy.'

'That electrician's a thief,' my mother-in-law commented.

Sure he is, I thought.

'I know a good electrician,' Arthur wobbled.

Sure you do.

At the table, Selma started talking about the hydrogen bomb, just to irritate me. Often she asked me in a dogmatic voice if I wanted to move to Russia. I married a fascist. Sure I wanted to move to Russia. The further from her the better. She wore a tunic dress la Grace Kelly. Pinned to her chest was an I LIKE IKE button. He'd just been nominated for the '56 election and already my wife had a button. 'A hydrogen bomb is something terrible,' I tried to explain.

'What about the A-bomb?' Selma goaded me. 'You afraid of that too?'

I felt like a coward.

'You should fear God,' my father-in-law commented over a pitcher of chicken fat. That was good, coming from him. He thumped the heavy wooden table. There was food in his teeth. My mother-in-law held a dish in front of Selma's face. 'Eat,' she said like she was talking to a child, feeding her with a spoon. My mother-in-law was the boss with a spoon. She never left the house. Suddenly the telephone rang. 'Don't answer it,' my father-in-law barked.

My wife cleared the table. I could hear her in the kitchen stacking dishes. Later she brought a plate of cookies and five cups of tea, without saucers, into the living room on a tray. 'Is that the way to serve tea?' my mother-in-law complained. Arthur just sat on the couch gazing at his knuckles. Any minute he'd open his mouth. I jerked away in fright.

I needed a drink. But my father-in-law, who was big in speakeasies and bootleg during the Depression, never even offered me a snort. In desperation I went to the bathroom for a pull at the hip flask I carried. On the way, I thought of burying Arthur alive. I bit my nails, planning it. I had to calm down. I'd give myself a coronary. Already I had hypertension and fat around my heart. Although I was skinny and sleek.

The bathroom was relatively cool with tiled walls. I ran the cold water and splashed my face. Tilting the flask to my mouth, I caught a glimpse of myself in the mirror. I was a handsome devil despite my shallow shifty face. I began to breathe easily.

Feeling much more relaxed, I returned to the living room. Arthur looked at me without moving or blinking an eyelid. He'd seen me in a Manhattan restaurant, when he dropped in to do their financial accounts. It was my bad luck. I was with another woman. Arthur was sitting at a table with an adding machine. He caught me kissing her in the darkened interior and nibbling her ear. This was some woman. I was head over heels. In the first place her name excited me: Marguerite. 'Oh Lord,' she kept saying with relish, playing with my fingers, even after I noticed Arthur and tried to edge away from her.

When Arthur offered to wash the dishes for his mother, which was unusual for him, I made my move. Calmly, I followed him into the kitchen and shadowed him to the sink. My wife had neatly arranged the dirty plates and glasses on the countertop. I picked up a stack.

As Arthur washed, it gave me some satisfaction to bring him not only dirty dishes, but clean ones as well. I rooted them out of the cupboards. Old dishes. Locked and rotting dishes. Cobwebby, coarse, many-sided and large. Sickroom dishes for invalids. It was my revenge. While Arthur, the creep, bent over the sink, I brought outrageous dishes to him. He never realised. Poor creep. Bobbing his hands up and down in the soapy water. Even when he washed a bedpan, he didn't get it. The whole time, he never complained. When he bent his head concentrating, I touched the back of his neck above his collar with the tip of my finger, teasing him. He didn't notice. He was too busy going round and round each plate with a wadded sponge. Then he attacked a burnt roasting tin with a hobnailed scourer.

I was taller than he was. I looked down disdainfully at his petty and humdrum ears as he tightened his grip on another soapy plate. He soaped it again and again. Water ran off the draining board onto the floor. I crept up behind him with a heavy casserole and raised it over his head. I could hear his even, balanced breathing. I took a practice swipe, whispering his name. The air churned around us. I steadied myself for the big one. High up on the kitchen ceiling, the electric lights buzzed. My mother-in-law flitted past the door.

'What's taking so long?' She peered into the windowless room.

Map makers are always secretly in love with what lies beyond the line.

The Mapmaker

They call me 'The Mapmaker,' because I got a youthful reputation as a careful planner. When I plan a job, I do it right! Now I got a situation at work that needs a cool-headed scheme. But instead of thinking, I'm biting my nails. Think shrewd, I remind myself. Think crooked.

Last week, a kid comes to me, says he wants to learn the ropes. This kid, who's connected through his uncle, is waiting for me to retire. Then he's going to take over my entire operation. His uncle's a Tsar. He controls an army in the Bronx. From a hot bath, he runs the whole borough. There's nothing I can do. You don't argue with a Tsar. Those who argue slip from walls, roofs and scaffolding.

This morning, I find the kid sitting on my desk, talking on my phone. Right away, my stomach starts to churn. Since he's joined the operation, I got ulcers. The office, let's face it, is a dump. We're over a diner. Frying sounds come up through the floor. Cockroaches you wouldn't believe. Waterbugs the size of a baby's foot. Woodticks. Horntails. Silverfish.

Two men follow me in. They're my overcoats. They go where I go. One of the coats carries my briefcase. He used to be a floorman in Havana. He never lets that case out of his sight. The other coat's a weight-lifter. He holds a sap under his arm. With his free hand, he dusts my chair. Then he touches the light switch, closes the blinds. The coats don't like this kid either. But what can they do? He's connected. They look at me. My hands are tied. I don't want to step on any big feet. I'm seventy-two years old for christssake. I have to hold my head tight to keep from doddering. I get these headaches sometimes. A ghost on legs with a cigarette, that's me.

When the kid sees us, he hangs up quick. 'Hiya Map,' he goes.

'It's Mister Moe Goldfarb to you.'

How's this kid got into my office? 'Get off my desk. That's fawn marble,' I say, crossing the room.

He's holding my collection book. I glare at him. My desk and tool-made chair are expensive. It's a crap room otherwise. A brown sink in one corner, blood-spatter marks showing through the paintwork on the walls, folding stools and TV tables. The front door's steel plated. It would take a locksmith to open it. Leaded windows. Wallsafe. Number-coded storage bins. Only I know the system.

I squint around. I got oldster eyeglasses I won't wear. Then I skate to the desk. (In my dreams.) The sun is coming up over the buildings outside. It muscles through the slats in the blinds. By ten o'clock the room's like a furnace. But the kid wears a black jacket, zipped up. Maybe he's got a narcotics habit. 'Man,' he complains. 'Who's the landlord? Somebody oughta red-cloth that crook. Don't you get no air? New York summers, huh?'

'What do you want, a building inspector up here?'

The kid's not too bright. He doesn't even have enough imagination to worry. He's a poor planner, I can tell. One step up from the coats. When he laughs, I see his mean little teeth. Soon he's going to start talking about Florida.

His uncle wants to retire me and my wife Gertrude to Miami Beach. Something relaxing for our golden years. I can't go to Florida. What about my girlfriend Rose? She needs a mink. Her son Winston? He needs a firm hand. There's my own son Arthur to look after and my daughter Selma. I got commitments in New York. I take out a bottle of Pepto Bismol. Unscrew the lid. Chug it down. Florida, if I go quiet. Otherwise, it's Jersey. In New Jersey I'll be looking up a lamppost.

'My uncle thinks maybe you need a rest,' the kid starts right in, frying me up like a chicken. I shrug, as if it doesn't matter to me one way or another. Finally, he discards his jacket. Underneath he's wearing a shiny girl's shirt that hangs outside his pants. His face is skinny as a skull. His eyes look crazy. His hands are limp. 'Take a holiday why don't you.' He makes his voice climb. The coats yuck. But I hear something threatening in the kid's tone and my guts burn.

'I have work to do.' I try to wave him away. Jerky, old-guy hand gestures. Then I get this pain in my side. Maybe it's gallstones.

The kid's called Brad. He walks over to the radiator and taps it. 'You got heat in August. What a dump,' he whines. Meanwhile I'm trying to think. Brad's related to people with pull. I nod my head like I'm considering the Florida deal. But I'm not ready to go. Not yet. I don't want to kill this Brad. I just want to slump his shoulders and scare him off. So I got to have a plan. That's my skill, planning. Staring at him, I see a nothing. Not worth killing. Creepo ankle socks. Perforated shoes. What are his credentials? Picking up betting slips? Me, I got a legitimate business. Quick Loans. I got eighteen misty trees on the books. Crap like that in Connecticut. But here's this kid spying on my operation. Moving in. Any goof-ups, he's going to tell his uncle, the Tsar. His uncle's so bent and decrepit, he looks like he's carrying a load on his back. Why doesn't *he* retire? They call him 'The Iceman.' He don't ice by himself. Naturally. He orders the ice-ing. He runs the show.

Me, I'm careful. I'm organised. First thing in the morning, I check to see if the bedroom window's been jimmied. If they want to fray my towel, they've got to out-plan me. I look through the peephole. Use the back stairs. But go quietly? I ain't going.

Okay, an idea is forming in the rear of my mind. I start doodling, nothing fancy. I'm drawing it out.

Letting it happen. I put my hand deep inside my pocket and feel around. Lucky for me, the packet's still there. Then the phone rings. Once. Stops. From the street outside there's a whistle. Everyone freezes. The coats are in the office with me, but the kid's disappeared. 'Find him,' I yell in a hoarse voice.

One of the coats gets up and makes for the door. The youngster's in the outer office eating a danish. 'I want you in here, where I can see you,' I say to him. My voice sounds old, cracked. 'Don't go to sleep on me,' I tell the coats. They give each other spooked looks. Brad thinks this is funny. He's got a smirk on his face. A car door slams in the street. An engine starts up. The Havana coat stands on a packing crate and looks out between the slats of the venetian blinds. 'We're okay Map,' he says. 'We're fine.'

I sit doing paperwork for a solid hour. I have to hold the book close to my eyes. I squint at the numbers. In the end, I put on my reading glasses. A contract shakes in my hand. Under the desk, it's a bug parking lot. A silverfish scuttles across my shoes. When I look up, I see Brad standing in the corner. He's listening to one of those transistor radios. I can't really hear the music. But I watch him snapping his fingers, tossing his head. He don't know I'm watching. 'Turn that off,' I holler. I'm almost sure I can take him. Like pushing a button. He's just a kid in a girlie shirt. Skinny chest. No stomach.

I sit back inhaling hot air. Then I stretch out

stiffly across the desk, grab an ashtray that reads: MARTY'S PRIME RIBS and light a cigarette. I got very clean fingernails. A nail polish called oyster. Nobody knows the colour I dye my hair. I dress like a gentleman. Three piece wool suits, in winter, custom-made. Monogrammed shirts. Silk ties. A handkerchief in my breast pocket. Cufflinks. Wing tips. In summer, I wear seersucker.

The coats read the papers. Step on cockroaches, nightwhisks and monkflies. The place is a jungle. The kid turns off his radio. He says he's got an idea for expanding the business. It just came to him.

'What do you suggest?' I ask sarcastically. I take off the pinchy eyeglasses. Smoke twitches from my nostrils.

'We move out of Brooklyn for starters,' he replies. He seems to be speaking from a long way off.

'What?'

'We get out of Brooklyn.'

I nod like I can hear him this time. A cockroach walks across the top of my desk.

'In Manhattan we can rent a real office. Get a secretary. Show some muscle. Move some shit. Score big.' Brad stops to think. The coats are waking-up. Looking at him with interest and respect. Has he got them on his side? 'Hot slots,' he continues. 'Nudes. Dice tables. Action numbers. We set up a furnace. Make some pay-offs.'

'We?'

He's giving me a real pain across my buttocks. In my head, I'm preparing to crack his knuckles. Suck out his pockets. Splay his feet. The coats avoid me, even though I try to catch their eyes. I'm going to thin this kid's blood. I shake out my cigarette with a jerk. The kid looks innocent, but he's got a sheet for aggravated assault. The little sadist smiles at me. Then hands over a note. 'My uncle dictated a message on the phone this morning,' he says.

'Dictated, huh?'

Stomach cramps, double-time. Wind. Heartburn. I glance at the note and toss it to the coats. It seems like it's been scribbled by a child. 'It's official,' I announce. 'The kid's been made my assistant.' Instead of yucking, the coats act impressed. I can't put it off any longer. With a groan, I get to my feet, casting one big shadow across the floor, and stagger to the bathroom.

The bathroom's outside the office, down a dark hallway. When I get inside, I hook the door quick. Then I fumble for the string-pull dangling from a bulb and yank it. In my pocket, I find the creased-up square of paper and the razor blade I keep for emergencies. I love my work. I want to sit on top of the heap forever - so I begin chopping. For a moment, I worry - could cocaine go stale?

I get the blow started, leaning over the crummy sink. The first snort splits my sides. I do another line. When I straighten up, I feel a big surge of atomic fire.

Secretly in love with what lies over the line (power, energy, youth - mostly youth) I pop the lock. Like a young guy, a grub with a big neck, I'm ready to kick ass. I'm seeing things fast and bright. No kid's going to take this away from me. Suddenly I got muscle tone. I got energy. Standing up straight, I could be taller than the kid. I'll show him who's boss. Show them all. I hurry down the hall. When I crash through the inner office door, the kid turns to face me. Crossing the room, I step on a bug, a silverfish, and leave the mess feebly twitching its legs.

No longer feeling my stiff joints, I breeze up close to the youngster, pat him hard on the back, like he's my own son. I already know he isn't the brainy type. I push him in the chest with my fist. Hit him with my pot belly. I could also grab his kidneys. But I decide to use guile. I take out my silk handkerchief and slowly wipe my face.

'Graduated Law from Brooklyn College. Did you?' I'm teasing the little bastard. I'm not even sure he can read or write too good. He isn't one of those snot-nosed grinds like my son Arthur.

When he cringes away, I look at my watch. Stretch. Play him along. Then I feel an urge to move. I know I'm tougher than he is. But I have to show this little shit my iron. Yank the rumour that I'm on the skids. I bend over easily and pick up a snoutbeetle. I like my work. I don't want to lie in the sun in front of a Miami Beach motel, playing gin-rummy, shitting around. The large beetle squirms between my fingers. Turns its head from side to side. I hold it out for the kid to see. This is my empire. I press the beetle's shell, crack it. Something oozes over my fingers. I stand very close. The youngster looks on in distaste, slack-jawed, wary, like he's wising-up.

The coats gawk too. But I ignore them. It's only Brad that interests me. 'You still looking?' I ask him. The sun, falling on me from behind, warms my shoulders and the back of my neck. This is my moment. I put the smeared snoutbeetle in my mouth. Chew and try to swallow it. 'Kid?' I say working my words around the twisted bug like it's a meatball hero - 'You think you got the stomach for this job?'

The Moon

I wanted mom to be happy. Her life with Pop was difficult. That was why I tried so hard to please her. I wanted the family to be normal. I wanted everything to be fine. I was a tax accountant. She liked that. When I went freelance she worried. Would I make it? I had a reputation for being clever. I saved my clients dough. Three years, going on four, I began earning big time. I could see she was proud. I had restaurants, clothes manufacturers, dentists. Good clients. I worked hard. Maybe too hard. Lately mom had stopped being impressed. Whenever I saw her, she looked hurt. Pop must have been giving her a hard time. Once he tried to slam a door on her fingers.

When she asked me to come over, I didn't hesitate, although it was a work day. Her voice on the phone sounded strained. It's Pop, I assumed, wrongly.

'When are you going to get married?' she cried as soon as I walked in the door. I dropped my briefcase in the foyer. She was wearing bedroom slippers and a bathrobe. I followed her to the living room. A floor lamp was turned on, although it was the middle of a sunny afternoon. I was surprised at her abruptness. She usually brought me a coffee or a glass of juice. Her question surprised me too.

'Ma, I'm working too hard. I don't got time,' I said.

'You're not even looking?'

She sat down on the couch.

'When? When am I going to look? All day I see clients. When I get home, the phone's ringing. It's another client. 'Come quick,' he says. 'I got a letter from The Internal Revenue.'

She made a face. 'Arthur, sit here, next to me.' She patted the couch. We were alone in the apartment. My father was out doing a deal. Every morning, two men in big overcoats met him at the door. They were what he called 'protection.'

I got up, crossed the area rug and sat down beside my mother. I was wearing a nice three piece suit. Florsheims on my feet. I adjusted the knife-edge crease in my trousers. A large man like myself needs an experienced tailor. I got one, in the Bronx. A genius. Mom admired the material. Then she leaned over and picked a piece of lint off my lapel. 'You have such a good income,' she said. She looked, I dunno, tired.

'How you feeling?' I asked.

'Eh. So, so.'

'You got your headaches again? What does the doctor say?'

She waved her hand. 'What I got a doctor can't fix.'

'Is it Pop?'

She sighed. 'Your father's a brute. So what else is new? He gets angry. He can't control his temper. You see this.' She rolled up her sleeve and showed me a bruise on her forearm. 'Your father. We're talking. Moe gets excited. He grabs me. He has a point he's got to make. He's not trying to hurt. He just has a heavy touch. If he wanted to hurt, by now I'd be dead.'

Her words made me feel physically sick. Anxiously I studied her face. I was the only one who cared about mom. My sister Selma took after Pop. Now mom was telling me I'd let her down. I was bewildered. Ashamed.

'Forget about me.' She plucked at her bathrobe. 'I want to see you settled.'

Was she serious? 'I'm settled,' I said.

'Settled down.'

'What do you mean? I'm making a bundle.'

'Money? Who cares. You need a wife, children. That's what makes life complete. Believe me.'

'Is your life complete?' I asked without thinking.

'Me?' She looked pained. 'I got your father.'

Enough said.

'Your sister's got Ernie.' We both grimaced. Mom took a hankie out of her bosom. I stared at it in alarm. 'What are you, too picky?' Tears appeared in the corner of her eyes. 'You're too picky.' She daubed her eyes. 'I'm not going to last forever. When I'm gone, who's going to worry about you? Your father?' More tears ran down her thin cheeks. 'Your sister Selma's married three years now. What's the matter?' she sniffled. 'No one's good enough? What do you want? The moon?' She sat back and cried.

'I used to make you happy. You were proud of

me,' I spluttered.

'That's true.' Mom pulled herself together. 'But Arthur, you're thirty.' Suddenly she got worked up again. 'If you loved me you'd settle down. It's like a slap in the face you're not settled. Your sister's ashamed. She can't hold her head up in the street. She's got a brother who's a bachelor. In the beauty parlour, the girls ask her if you're married yet. They want to fix you up. But you don't even date. You hide behind a stack of cancelled cheques and whatnot. You're an attractive man. Prosperous. Artie.' My mother reached out for my hand. 'We made you an appointment.'

My blood ran cold. With the hairdresser? What did she want me to do? Have a perm? I was already thin on top.

'With who?'

'With a marriage broker, that's who. I'm burning for you to get married.' She showed me a newspaper clipping: THE ODETTE GELT MATRIMONIAL AGENCY.

I flinched. Looked around. It wasn't normal going to a marriage broker. I knew that.

'She's a broker. Like a stockbroker,' my mother said encouragingly. 'What's the big deal? I saw her ad in *The New York Post*. Look at the small print. *Marriage is an investment*,' my mother quoted from the clipping she'd saved. 'That ought to appeal to you. I already spoke to her. Over the phone she said she had a wide nuptial experience. You're going to see her tomorrow. Ten o'clock. Wear the suit. It makes you look nice.'

After seeing Odette Gelt, I wanted to go right home and die. But I had a business appointment I couldn't get out of - a lunchtime appointment with a restaurant owner who had tax nightmares. All I wanted to do was sit down and recover from Odette Gelt. I'd come directly from her office with a stack of photographs of marriageable girls I dared not look at. Maybe a marriage broker was a good thing, I was thinking. I'd been too busy to look for a wife. Time's money, right? Makes sense. Get someone else to sort it out.

The restaurant owner slapped me on the back as soon as I walked in the door. His dive was already losing. The place was deserted. It was a tax write-off. I could see this immediately.

'You're a genius,' he said, leading me to a table. He knew I could work magic with numbers. 'The office is a mess. You'll be more comfortable here. Have something to eat. It's on the house.'

The photographs from Mrs Gelt were in an envelope under my arm. My reputation was so great, the proprietor actually called the waiter and had him wipe down the chair with a towel. 'How'dya like that Ike?' he asked, giving me a wink and a nod while the waiter wiped. 'I hope he survives,' I said, stiffly. I meant, I hope President Eisenhower beats the pants off Adlai Stevenson. But I got it wrong. It sounded wrong. Why didn't I just say what I meant? I was no good at talking. I felt bulky in my three piece suit. I was jumpy and perspiring. If I didn't find a wife, I was finished, as far as my mother was concerned. She'd never forgive me. A man without a wife wasn't worth a damn.

I tried to get THE ODETTE GELT MATRIMONIAL AGENCY off my mind. But I couldn't do it. She had a small office with a couch, low lights and dainty furniture. From her advertisement, I'd imagined something more like a bank.

Mrs Gelt wore a lot of perfume. She showed me her testimonials. These were letters from happy couples she'd brought together. They were bound in a velvet-covered book. I pretended to smile while she took my details, noting, with pleasure, my salary. Then she looked through her files. 'You wouldn't believe how many women I got on file,' she told me. 'You want divorced?'

I was unsure. I hadn't even considered the possibility. 'I wouldn't mind widowed.' My throat had turned very dry. I swallowed hard. I didn't even know why I'd said that. Probably so I'd sound more fair-minded. The idea of a widow horrified me. I didn't want divorced either. Another phoney smile. My face felt stretched out. When I left, Mrs Gelt gave me a packet of photographs and told me to look through them at my leisure. Oh sure. Find a girl I liked.

I put the packet on the table and tried to get to work. Lifting my new portable adding machine out of its case, I positioned it near my right hand. I was ready. Just then the waiter came over and poured me a glass of water. 'Good afternoon,' he said in an English accent. I wasn't an ordinary customer. I barely looked up. Instead I forced myself to stare at a thick account book and a sheaf of tax forms.

I picked up my mechanical pencil. But I couldn't get into tax-accountant mode. I wanted to shower, shave, put on slacks and a clean shirt. It was the middle of the afternoon. I was sitting in a dark restaurant, a dive, in a hot suit. I was supposed to be working. I stabbed at a pile of papers with my pencil. Bills and invoices. I had to get started. But I couldn't start. I was usually all business. I loosened my tight collar. Undid my tie. Then I called the waiter. 'It's too dark,' I complained.

The guy brought me a candle. A candle, I ask you? I puffed myself up. Rubbed my forehead. Complained. He was a young guy. He shrugged. Looked sorry. Went off and got a small table lamp. Plugged it in. He was quick on his feet. Agile. I watched him with pleasure. I'm a big man. I admire agility in others. 'Would you like a drink?' he inquired. Normally I didn't drink on the job. I pulled my chair closer to the table. 'Just coffee.' Coffee? I needed a Pepto Bismol.

Systematically, I divided a stack of cancelled

checks into two piles and stared at the slick surface of the table between them. I tried to work. But the image of my mom in her bathrobe disturbed me. 'I'm not going to last forever,' she'd said. I remembered how her pale face lit up when I agreed to see Mrs Gelt.

'You win,' I whispered. Frantically, I reached under the tax flimsies, grabbed the packet of photos and tore it open. I put my hand inside, felt the slick surface of the top photograph, and shuddered. Then I moved my fingers to the edge. Without looking, I counted. There were four photos. Four women in all. I slid out the first one. My hand was shaking. Instead of looking at it, I pictured my mother's unhappy face. She was ready for a nervous breakdown. I took a deep breath. Squirmed in my seat. Then I lowered my eyes.

The first woman was pretty, but appeared tired and worn. I sat on the edge of my seat. There were bags under her eyes. My fingers trembled slightly. I was jittery and sad. The next woman had a dimpled, simpering expression on her fleshy face. I groaned without a sound. Is there still a chance for me? I wondered. The third woman looked sharp and thin. I imagined kissing her cheek. I felt shame and fear. On the back of the photographs were printed details, but I didn't want to know anything more about them. I turned the pictures over without even looking at the fourth one. I was too picky. This might mean that I'd never get married. I imagined my mother's anguished face.

In the furthest shadowy corner of the restaurant, a couple held hands. They were talking in whispers. When I noticed them, I felt like a drowning man, miserable and alone. Then, the waiter approached with my coffee. As he put down the cup, his fingers brushed mine. 'Thank you,' I said in my formal, stiff way. He placed milk, sugar, a napkin and a spoon in front of me. Underneath the table, my legs started to shake. 'I'm feeling fine,' I told myself, adding milk and sugar to the cup. I took a sip. 'Nice caugh-fee,' I called out to him. What a dope I was. While I drank, I watched the young waiter. The restaurant was slow, almost empty, but I could tell by the way he moved that he was efficient. I followed his slim posterior with my eyes. Was he a dancer? He moved so gracefully. He had a slight build I found precious. Resting my eyes on him, the word *boodle* came back to me, from childhood. It was the baby word my sister Selma and I were given for buttocks. It made me laugh.

Feeling optimistic, I picked up the photos again. Only one left to look at. I took it out of the stack and studied it, image side down. This was going to be the one. On the smooth back, I read the woman's name, *Flo Hirschorn*. Crouching forward, eager, I held my breath, turned the paper over and looked. Another clunker.

'What do you want? The Moon?' I heard my mother's voice in my head. I touched my lips with my napkin. The moon was pearly, full, half-round or crescent-shaped. Sometimes it glistened. When I raised my head, the waiter caught my eye. He'd returned with a menu. I hadn't asked for a menu. I stared at him. He had a small, rosebud mouth and a strong, cynical expression. He pouted, smiled. 'Anything else you want?' he inquired. Overcome with fear and longing, I gazed into his questioning face.

I wanted a woman like him.

Little Bird

I got out of bed in a state of confusion. The clock on the table I used said eight. I must have slept, but I didn't feel rested. I forced myself to get dressed. I could have stayed in bed all day. Outside the window, it was grey and seemed to be getting greyer. Could it be eight o'clock at night? I tried to think back. I didn't believe I had to go to work today. Today was Sunday.

After tossing and turning, I remembered finally falling into a doze - when a loud noise roused me. Now that I was awake, I realised it was coming from above. It was a heavy, thudding sound like someone moving furniture. My upstairs neighbours again. Soon the thumping music would start. Often they ran their washing machine late into the night and I was disturbed by the mechanical whirring and spinning. I didn't believe they had carpets on their floors. Sometimes their little girl bounced a ball - indoors.

Staggering to the bureau, I brushed past the pile of empties I'd left in plain view on my bedside table. Without turning on a light, because I didn't think my eyes were up to it, I hunted for my underwear. In the dim glow from the window, I chose nylons and a slip. Then I perched on the bed again. From upstairs I could hear objects falling or being hurled around. Tentatively, I stretched out one long foot and flexed my toe. Then I bent over groaning and eased on my stocking.

When I heard their Elvis music starting up, something heavy rose inside me. I felt a rush of sweat. It was all I could do to keep from falling back against the pillows. Since the neighbours moved in upstairs, I hadn't had a decent night's sleep. I used to sleep like a lamb. The building where I lived in New York City had always been a relatively quiet place. There were twelve floors and only eight apartments per floor. Modest these days compared to the new high-rises.

I swallowed experimentally. My mouth was very dry. Inside I had that choked-up feeling I sometimes got. It was like my chest bones were too large and were pressing on my skin. My thin flesh felt tight. This tight dryness was made worse by the central heating system. It was regulated from a distant boiler and I couldn't turn it down or off. The only thing I could do was open the window and suffer commotion from the street below. I was convinced the radiators had hidden controls. Once I got on my hands and knees and tried to peck around behind the bedroom unit. I was looking for a small wheel to turn, a button to press or something to push to an *off* position. I should have complained, but I didn't like to bother the management. I didn't like to bother anyone. I prized myself on my hard-won self-sufficiency.

After I got the other stocking up, I stood abruptly. But their grating, grinding music knocked me back again. It was far too loud. There was a rhythmic booming. Lyrics I could actually understand, but didn't like, blasted into my bedroom. I only wanted to sit down and shut my eyes. Maybe wet my lips. I hated that family. There was a sleek, dark father whom I rarely saw. The mother had a sloppy appearance. There was one brat. The girl looked about seven, but she might have been older. She was small and scrawny. I think there was a baby now. Frequently I heard a baby cry.

Once I got my bedside table tidied, I went into the bathroom and washed my face. In the bathroom mirror, I looked old and tired. When I wiped my wet face with a towel, my poor skin felt raw. The noise from above was, if anything, even louder. I couldn't believe the nerve of those upstairs neighbours. I clung to the sides of the porcelain sink, feeling my blood pressure rise. Staggering only a little, I flapped down the short hall to the kitchen. From the cupboard where I kept the ironing board, I got out my broom. Then I returned to the bathroom. I held the broom down near the bristles, reached over my head, and banged the handle several times on the ceiling, hollering 'Shurr-up!' as loud as I could. By now, my whole ceiling was mussed with black marks from where I'd hit it with the broom handle in the past.

The music was so loud I don't think they heard me banging and screaming. At the sink I took a couple of extra-strength aspirins and washed them down with water I drank directly from the tap. That's when I started thinking of the countryside.

I was born in the city; I'd lived all my life in the

city, but I suddenly remembered the peace of the country. I had a cousin who still lived there. When I was young, I used to be sent off to visit with her and my aunt and uncle in the summertime, when my mother got fed up and was so unwell she had to visit the drying-out clinic. I remembered the quiet nights and the bright stars.

Landing for a moment on the toilet, because I was a bit light- headed, I followed this memory. For a while, I felt more peaceful than I had in days, except for my arid throat. I tried to remember the rolling farmland that surrounded my cousin's house. There was one paved road. Along this road were dairy farms. There were cornfields. I liked to flit around without shoes. I remembered it as the time my poetic nature was formed. But it wasn't all that idyllic.

One day, my cousin Mary led me to a haunted house, which was down a dirt track, overgrown with gloomy pines. It had just rained. Small lizards collected in the puddles. They always came out after the rain. Cousin Mary picked one up and held it by its tail, dangling it in front of my face. I didn't want to touch it, so I cringed away. I knew it would be wet and cold - and for a moment I was so disturbed, I thought of my mother in the clinic. This distasteful feeling was all mixed up with an overwhelming sense of excitement and anticipation about the house we were going to see, a painful thrill that was almost pleasure - but really, I knew nothing about pleasure and pain in those days.

At an overgrown clearing, my cousin led me, chirruping behind her, off the road and into some thorny bushes. I was used to city streets and the deep, dark countryside away from roads and familiar landmarks began to frighten me. 'How much further is it?' I asked. It was so quiet, I could hear the humid heat humming in the trees. We walked a bit more and I knew I would never find my way back to the track without Mary. I kept very close to her. When she stopped to pick something round and dusty off a bush and offer it to me, I edged away. 'Aren't you hungry Flo?' When I didn't respond, she put the berry in her own mouth and began chewing and making satisfied noises. I knew she was not above tricking me. She'd done so in the past, fooling me into eating things that weren't wholesome. I was small and thin, white-faced with dark eyebrows, still bird-hipped and tiny. Sometimes I had a frightened expression, but when I smiled, I was beautiful, like my mother.

We crossed an open field. I thought of all the different kinds of birds in the world. Eventually, through some straggly trees, I saw the abandoned house Mary was leading me to. It was made of wood that had turned green. The front porch sagged. The roof had holes in it and some of the dark windows were broken.

Feeling very young, I stood close to my cousin. When she crossed the threshold, I was at her heels.

The interior was gloomy and cool. It smelled of earth and something else, something sharp I couldn't identify. Together we walked down a long hall. There were dry leaves on the floor inside. We rustled through them. At the end of the hall, we entered what was left of a kitchen.

At any moment, I was ready to fly. The muscles in my legs burned in anticipation of a fast exit. The back of my neck prickled. 'They were rubbish,' Mary said. 'The folks who lived here.'

I nodded, looking around the large kitchen. There wasn't much left of them: their big old table in the middle of the room and a broken cooking pot on a listing counter. Taped to one wall, a faded magazine photograph of a movie star with dark, exotic looks and full lips made me sad. There were animal droppings on the floor. In one corner, I noticed sheets of newspaper. They'd turned the colour of something that had been roasted in an oven. I bent close. Mostly the pages were hard to comprehend, but I did read the name CAPONE. I think it was then that I felt panic overwhelm me. Raising my head, I noticed Mary had left the room. She was stomping up the stairs in search of the bedrooms. I wanted to catch hold of her feet. I was frightened that she would fall suddenly through the floorboards. I felt physically sick. Then I didn't care about Mary. I just had to be out of that house.

As I was hurrying back down the hall, I passed a half-closed door I hadn't noticed before. I nudged it open with the toe of my shoe and looked in. There on the wall, right in front of me, hung a little bird with its wings spread. I stepped closer, although my heart was pounding and my pulse was racing. It was a brown sparrow. Fascinated, I moved closer still. A nail had been driven into the wall right through each little wing.

My eyes flew open and I looked around the bathroom where I sat. I retched and gagged. Thumping sounds and screams echoed from above. 'That's it!' I said out loud, getting to my feet. I could still see the crucified bird, as if it were hanging, over thirty years later, on my bathroom wall, crumbling to rotten shreds. I grabbed the door frame to steady myself. I felt the bird beating its wings in my throat.

In my bedroom, I threw a robe over my slip and put shoes on my feet. I didn't care that my hair was ruffled and that I wasn't even wearing make-up. On second thought, I grabbed a lipstick and applied it, using a corner of the window as a mirror. I was in a hurry. My hand was shaking. On my way out the door, I disturbed a brown paper sack that stood ready to be taken to the incinerator. It was filled with empty bottles and, when they fell over behind me, I could hear them rattling, but not breaking, as they rolled out onto the parquet.

I ran up a flight of stairs and found myself standing in front of my neighbours' door. I was burning with anger. I clutched my robe to my throat and rang the bell. Pulling myself tightly together, I waited. The hallway seemed eerily quiet and I imagined I could hear my own heart beat. What had happened to the loud music they'd been playing? Surely it would have echoed into the hall. But I could hear nothing. Not even the scraping sounds that signify the end of a record, setting my teeth on edge. Nothing but my own nervous heart. I rang the bell again. 'It's your neighbour, Flo Hirschorn.'

A moment later, the door opened cautiously. A young girl stood on the threshold. 'Listen to me,' I began to say. I recognised her as the daughter of the wretched family who moved furniture, played records and ran the washing machine at all hours of the day and night.

'My mama's not home,' she quaked.

Her cheeks were white and, when she turned her face up towards mine, I recognised a familiar pleading expression. To tell the truth, it embarrassed me. I don't know why I did it; I didn't mean it to happen, but studying her, I started to cry.

Gertie And Moe

Gertie is seventy-five years old. When her husband, Moe, becomes pale one afternoon and clutches his chest, she's frightened. Suffering herself from agoraphobia, brought on and aggravated over the years by Moe's dangerous profession, she thinks he should be retired by now. But he's still making deals.

'Moe?' She looks over at him. 'Are you short of breath?'

'It's nothing.' He doesn't want to be disturbed. He's on the phone with his shady partner - arguing, pleading, threatening- and trying to ignore the frightening way he feels, like feathers are floating inside him, slowly drifting towards a blockage. He's a small-time gangster, very dapper and crooked. He looks younger than his years and still considers himself a spring chicken. In their tomb-like apartment, his face glows white. What if he should die?

After he hangs up the phone, Moe asks for a sip of water. But there is no water. Due to a municipal shortage, the result of political mismanagement and a serious summer drought, the taps in New York City are dry for all but an hour a day. She knows this, but Gertie heads for the kitchen sink anyway. She is small and frail, with a bent back and a little, white, female mustache. In blind and hopeless desperation, she turns on the cold tap. There is a distant belching and gurgling like the noises Moe has begun to make in the next room. But otherwise, nothing. She opens the fridge. Only prune juice. Maybe he'll drink prune juice. She finds a glass. It pours brown and thick as old blood. Moe can't even manage the merest swallow.

When Gertie phones for an ambulance, they ask if it's an emergency, and she says, 'Well, yes.' Maybe she should phone the children. Selma and Arthur have their own lives but they'd want to know. Moe is lying on the couch, his collar opened and his tie undone.

'Come with me,' he cries out in a hoarse frightened voice. For a terrible moment, she thinks he means to the grave. She has no choice. She gets dressed. For years she's worn nothing but a housecoat and slippers. Her clothes, hanging in plastic bags, feel stiff and new. The colours are unfamiliar. In a daze, she puts on a skirt and blouse smelling of mothballs.

One of the ambulancemen calls Moe, 'Pops,' but avoids looking in his eyes. The other is very handsome, Gertie cannot help but notice, sleek-faced, with an Elvis Presley hairdo. Outside, the street is bright and hot. Foliage has died from lack of water. Nevertheless, Gertrude finds it, at first, beautiful. Great changes have taken place while she's been indoors. The sight of the sidewalk, a lampost, the neighbours, makes her gasp. In the ambulance, she holds Moe's hand, regretting, all of a sudden, the years cut off from life. Lying on the sofa, reading romance books with a large magnifying glass, her legs have become numb. When she looks down now she notices, with a start, the shoes she's wearing. They are white with peep-toes and wedge-shaped heels. She's worn slippers for a decade. Her feet feel pinched and sore. But the white shoes make them appear shapely and young. She's always had nice ankles and legs.

Moe looks old and worn. He has cash hidden in various safe deposit boxes in banks around the city. In a slurred and cracking voice he tries to tell her about these and other secret stashes. But Gertie can't make out what's being said to her. His business has broken her spirit. His philosophy of life has sometimes been brutal. Now his head keeps dropping to one side. His hair, carefully combed and oiled straight back from his brow, is dishevelled. She lifts his hand to her lips. 'Get better,' she whispers. And, 'I'm sorry.' She thinks about the doctors who are waiting in the hospital to rejuvenate him. She thinks about slippers and shoes. She remembers the love letters he'd once written to her. As they approach a busy intersection in the wild, dry city, the ambulance siren wails. A tube of pure air dangling overhead jiggles when they pick up speed again.

'After you get well, we'll go dancing,' Gertie promises.

Unfortunately, Moe dies.

Where Is The Air Coming In?

I came from Long Island on the spur of the moment. Now I wished I'd stayed home. Scheming, I thought I could talk to Arthur. I needed someone to talk to. Problems with my husband were overwhelming me. I had my bags already packed. I was stupid with unhappiness. Would Arthur know what to do? Probably not. I didn't kid myself. My big brother knew nothing about life. Although he was a good accountant, all he did was work, scooping up money. One of his clients was Governor Dewey's cousin. 'How come you make so much money?' I once asked him. I could have been the brains in the family. 'It's a gimmick,' he said. Still, I trusted him. He knew my husband, Ernie. There were things I wouldn't have to explain.

In my handbag I carried my empty savings account book. Arthur had money to spare. Right away I'd be grateful. I could die seeing myself like this. A million problems were eating me up inside. I got these headaches sometimes. If I didn't tell someone soon, I was going to burst. I was going to get really sick. I was going to blow my stack. I guess I wanted to leave Ernie. The person I should have told was my mother. Lately she'd been looking at me like she already knew. But I didn't want to add to mom's troubles. She had dad. My father would kill Ernie if he realised how unhappy I was. Or have him killed.

Arthur's swanky building looked like a bank. The lobby had picture windows and shiny walls. The overhead lights were glaring. This was the opposite of the shadowy tenement where we grew up, when dad was just starting out. There was flat grey carpet on the floor and rows of slick chrome mailboxes in Arthur's building. In the glare of the overhead lights, I noticed a run in my stockings. My dreamboat coat? Forget it. The very least it needed was a dry-cleaning. I used to be smart, vivacious. People used to refer to me as a live-wire. I even had an excitable bladder. At the moment, my jacked-up hair was wild and wind-blown like Anna Magnani's. I needed a cut and set. My hairdo was murder.

A man in a uniform stood in the doorway, rubbing his cold hands together and staring at his feet. When I entered, he followed me into the lobby and motioned me over to a desk. On the desk sat a telephone and a sign that said, NO SCUM, PEEPERS, SHARKS, OR BARFLIES. I swear to God.

'Are you expected Ma'am ?' he asked

I wasn't.

'What's the apartment number ?' He picked up his telephone.

'Can't I give my own brother a surprise? Just this once,' I begged. I should have brought a Jell-O salad or something. I passed him a crumpled five spot I couldn't afford. 'Okay,' the guy nodded, laying his hand on the rim of his cap. 'But don't tell no one.'

Arthur's bad-news apartment building was called THE EXECUTIVE. Standing in front of the elevators, I tried to think how I could talk to him. My brother didn't invite confidences, believe me. I suspected my husband Ernie was seeing another woman. Once I heard him sobbing in the bathroom. Another time, I picked up the telephone extension and heard him say, 'Please, Marguerite,' in a despairing voice. I already felt like the wronged wife. I qualified. I did a test in a magazine. Ernie was exhibiting all the signs. I was convinced. Lately when we kissed, he kept his mouth closed. First sign.

Before leaving the house, I took a Bufferin. My husband was a nothing. He borrowed from anyone he could put the bite on. We had zip. This Marguerite must have been desperate. Ernie was losing his business, hitting the skids. His credit was lousy. Guys came to the house and repossessed our car. After they drove away in our new 1956 Buick hardtop, Ernie said he was going to hang himself with a belt. Thank God we still had the furniture. If daddy knew, Ernie would be dead. A guy with a big neck, round, fast and smooth, would waste him.

On the Long Island Rail Road this morning, I bought another sapbrain magazine. I looked through it, bug-eyed, for advice. Getting wise to myself, I called it. I thought I would never stop hurting. When we were married, Ernie was young and handsome. Mister Right? Yeah right. At present, I was only twenty-four years old. I still wanted sloppy, openmouthed kisses.

Impatiently I pressed the *up* button. Then a middle middle aged woman joined me. She looked harmless enough. A large woman, cold and pale. Quietly, but expensively dressed. When the elevator arrived, we both walked in. I was riding for a fall, but I didn't know it. The souped-up carriage was all silver and white like the inside of a cocktail shaker. It ran automatically, without an operator. Frankly, I was glad the woman was there because I didn't know how to do self-service. The walls were polished. The control panel was brushed. When you pushed your floor, an orange number lit up, causing my red-rimmed eyes to clench. My head was pounding. I should have used the stairs. But Arthur lived on the seventeen floor with a view of the George Washington Bridge.

The woman kept it zipped, but as soon as the doors hissed closed, she turned to me. Her wise-guy eyes squinted open and her hair seemed to stand up a little on her head. 'Excuse me,' she said and started pointing to her feet. 'Want to see something?' she beckoned me close. 'I got killer boils. Ever see a boil this big? Bet you think it's a bunion. It's not.' With a groan, she lifted her shoe. Through a slit in the leather, up near the toe, an inflamed swelling protruded.

I parked my carcass in the corner as far as I could get from her. 'It's full of fluid.' She followed me with a lurch, like Mrs Frankenstein. 'Tell me, is it oozing?'

Grimacing, I turned away and dug my head down into my collar. This was murder. I couldn't understand how my brother lived here. It was a nice new building, with a view of the palisades, but full of bad-news people like this gal.

'A hot compress every two hours used to help.' Mrs Frankenstein gazed at her own foot in awe. 'Look here.' She tried to clutch my arm. 'They've got to open it with a sterile needle. Then they're going to get out the surgical knife.'

I didn't say a word, so she continued, pressing close. 'The boil I had before this was a real monster,' she went on. 'Black around the edges, it twisted and dropped off. I didn't need surgery for that one. I picked it out of the carpet.'

'Jesus,' I lurched back. Did this gal have no dignity? She swayed close, her face stretched wide, sucking up all the breathable air. I needed a minute to think out my strategy. Instead I was harassed. I didn't feel I could just jump into this with Arthur. I had to play it smart. My brother made a good income. I wanted him coughing-up.

Looking anywhere but at my travelling companion and her feet, I began to feel hot. There was pressure on my throat as if I was choked. I gazed around for a ventilation hole. Where was the air coming in? I panicked, hot-spots on my cheeks. Maybe I would die here.

When the elevator stopped at her floor, the woman quit shooting her mouth off and got out. She stepped out demurely. Not like a woman with boils.

On the seventeenth floor, I walked down a long, featureless corridor, lit up a bright grey. When I got to Arthur's, I felt queasy and doomed. I rang the bell. Arthur, the big cheese, answered. He was wearing an orlon cardigan. I shot in. His large stomach protruded. He patted his hair and frowned. My brother was neat and cared about good furniture, but I was so upset, I couldn't appreciate a thing he'd done with the interior decorating. I just wanted to sit down and start talking. I had this image of him taking pity on me and shelling out. He laughed his big, false-hearty laugh. Maybe it was already too late. If he noticed I'd been crying, he didn't let on. Instead, he took my old coat. Boy was I embarrassed about that coat. Seeing dollar signs, I gave Arthur a kiss on the cheek, which he didn't return.

'What a surprise,' he said, raising his eyebrows. Poor, dumb, lonely Arthur. He touched my elbow and I had the urge to sob out my confession in the foyer. Just then the bedroom door opened wide and a slender, dark-haired, boyish man walked into Arthur's living room. 'This is Tony,' my brother said. He made a helpless, stretching motion with his big, awkward hands as he introduced us. Tony was barefoot.

Tony? I looked at him and kept looking. He was

bunching his shirt into his trousers. Through the open bedroom doorway I saw Arthur's fat wallet lying on the bureau.

Arthur and I sat close together on his expensive living room couch. Boyish Tony sat in an armchair opposite. It was almost dusk. 'So Selma, how's Ernie?' my stupid brother asked.

'Great,' I said.

Arthur once told me he admired Ernie's nerve. Ernie was waiting for a letter or a cheque. Whenever the phone rang, I was supposed to say, 'No, he's not here.'

Outside, the shadows were gathering. Tony turned on a light. He hadn't said a word yet. From the window, I could see New Jersey. A Tip-Top bread sign glowed pink against the sky. Otherwise, it looked cold and bare at this hour of the day. When my brother went into the kitchen to make coffee, I followed the tread of his heavy shoes, trying to work up some nerve. There's plenty of time, I told myself. I asked for a seltzer. 'I got to tell you,' I started to say, but I couldn't continue.

Arthur had a big bottom, a straight back, and fleshy hips. He took something out of the freezer. Then he turned and looked at me. I used to be a happy woman. Sinking back against the kitchen counter, I hoped he'd notice the change, but he didn't comment. I also kept quiet. How could I say anything with Tony, cool and sneaky, listening in the next room? Forget the bankbook. The bankbook was out of the question now. While Arthur took out his good china, light, thin-edged cups and saucers, I felt my neck sink down between my shoulders. To hell with it, I almost turned on the waterworks. I could get so upset, I'd have to lie down. Then I imagined myself in my brother's bedroom, scrabbling through his wallet.

Arthur carried a tray into the living room. Tony hadn't moved. We sat down again. The couch had transparent, zippered, plastic covers. I shifted uneasily. Fumbling, I put a cigarette between my lips. Tony jumped up and lit it with his Zippo. Over the flame, his eyes met mine. Never mind the hard times, his dark eyes said. Or so I thought.

'May I?' He took one of my cigarettes for himself. I thought his voice sounded phoney, but I liked him anyway. I sat back and tried to relax. There was something I was missing. I let the coffee run over my tongue and sifted it against my teeth making a slurping noise. But my eyes were clouded and I couldn't see straight. Everything was smoke. Suddenly I heard a shout and thought it might have come from my own mouth. But it was some hopped-up guy yelling seventeen floors below in the street. The whole city was yelling.

It must have been cool in Arthur's apartment, because my knees started shaking. I crossed my legs. Something was dying in me. It was a strange, thick feeling. I didn't say a word. I wanted to speak to my brother alone. Arthur was always alone. Except for now. Now his eyes were shining. He drank his coffee in sips. His hands were too big for his cup.

'Tony's a waiter,' Arthur said. His cheeks lifted. 'He's English.'

'From England?' I hunched my shoulders. I'd never met anyone from England before. Was Tony a client? Of course not. My brother's friend propped his naked feet on the ottoman in front of him and wiggled his long toes. There was an atmosphere I couldn't understand.

Normally, I talked like a maniac. I could eat a sandwich in four bites. Even Arthur must have known something was wrong. At the door, he tried to hug me. He hardly ever touched me before. Moving uncertainly, his expensive clothes loose and rumpled, he stopped to get his balance, then leaned towards me again. 'I'll call,' he said.

So much for my needling scheme. Have a nice life, I thought, as I left him.

The down elevator was empty except for me and a wizened old man with a long nose. 'My husband Ernie's cheating. He's gone outside the marriage. We're broke,' I said to this old guy, a complete stranger, as soon as I heard the automatic doors shut.

'Life stinks,' I shouted, swooping with anger.

The old man looked over at me fearfully. There was a rolled-up newspaper in his hand. As the elevator broke loose and descended, it snapped against his leg.

Dowsing In The North East Of England

Marguerite was used to more adventurous partners. In truth, adventurous men also made her miserable, but it was a different kind of misery. In New York City she'd had a string of affairs with sharpies from Brooklyn who two-timed her with other girlfriends, and wives. Marriage to Colin was supposed to have been her revenge. They met in New York. After they became engaged, he took her back to England where they were married. Colin was a trainee dentist. He talked about nothing but saving money. He said they were skint. Sometimes, to vary the conversation, he told stories about teeth and horrible oral conditions that required surgery. She listened avidly for a while. When she first came to Britain, thinking she had a future as a wife, she packed away her attitude, along with her New York style stilettos, her blood red lipsticks and wild gardenia perfume. Recently she'd fetched everything out again.

Towering over the other customers in her high heel shoes, she pointed past slabs of dripping, bones and hocks to a trussed chicken turning golden on a spit behind the butcher's counter. 'I'll have that one,' she said in her strong New York accent. 'I've had a rotten winter.'

The butcher looked up amazed as he wrapped her chicken in greaseproof paper and popped it into a brown bag. His skinny assistant came out of the fridge wearing an anorak. He looked at Marguerite, then cowered away. A wireless played behind them. Over the till was a photograph of a man in uniform kneeling beside a whippet. 'The weather's set fine,' the wireless said, 'with temperatures at a record high for the month of May.'

Following this, a report from a place called Suez announced that a canal was about to be reopened to navigation. The butcher winked at Marguerite. 'A special occasion hinny? This'll be a treat for the family. Can I interest you in some black pudding today?' His eyes were a watery, icy blue that turned grey in shadow like the North sea.

Marguerite paid with the rent money. She looked into the mirror of a display cabinet and touched her hair. It was wavy and gleaming. 'Yeah right,' she said and strode out of the shop. 'Don't make me laugh,' she murmured, feeling his wet eyes behind her.

She'd already bought a fresh stottie cake, and some very expensive green grapes. A puny fruit and veg man packaged the bunch sorrowfully in newspaper, assuming she was taking them to an invalid. He'd also failed to understand, his voice solemn and slow as if the invalid were already dead. In his tiny shop, her fingers felt the size of bananas. Over the door, a fragile balsawood model of a Spitfire still dangled. As she left, she gave it a vigorous shake. Striding like a colossus down the narrow, Northern streets, Marguerite wondered if she needed cheese. In New

York she never thought of cheese. She danced on tables, light as air. She lived! Stopping short, she told herself to wise-up. It wasn't all dancing. There were occasions when she was swallowed by darkness there.

The rest of the rent money flew out of her hands. She was determined to have a special day. Dairy products caused her to bloat, but at this point she didn't care. 'I'm going to swell like a sow,' she told the cheese man who blushed, frisking at her heels to the very threshold of his shop. His wife peeped from an interior door, drawn by Marguerite's American voice.

She was magnificent. Tear-bright eyes, good skin. There had just been time to buy a bit of Wensleydale before the bus. She held the heavy English coins lightly. There was warmth in the air today and the sun was shining. She pulled her dark curls back, then shook them forward. A young man carrying a sack of coal stopped and stared at her.

At the station, she got a coach headed out of the city. She'd booked a day trip to a ruined castle beside the sea. Her purse was nearly empty and Colin would be furious. Perhaps she'd never go home again.

Poor Colin, labouring on teeth in the dental hospital, tightening the forehead clamp used to keep patients immobile in his treatment chair, knew nothing of her plans. 'They faff about,' he told her once when she asked about the seat.

'Isn't that cruel?'

'I know.' He made a sad face.

Colin thought she was at home wringing out his shirts because she didn't have an automatic washing machine. Even her mother in Bensonhurst had an automatic. Colin's mother in Blyth beat clothes in a metal bucket with a heavy piece of wood until she got her twin tub. Once a week, they went to her house for Sunday dinner. 'Marguerite cannot cook,' Colin told his mother, morosely. His mother was just waiting for her to 'fall wrong.'

Although it was a Saturday, the humped, pre-war bus was not full. The passengers were all oldsters, a few with cameras around their necks. Marguerite avoided them. They were just shapes to her. A hazy featureless old man was already asleep, his head sunk like a weight between his shoulders. As she walked carelessly down the aisle with her picnic, her wide skirt brushing the seats, some heads raised. The smell of roast chicken filled the bus.

At the back, sitting alone on the aisle, an elegant young man barely stirred. She couldn't help but notice him. His long tortured face, high cheekbones and arrogant expression made her heart beat quicker. His handsome looks alone sent her into oblivion. The moment she saw him, she knew. He stood and let her have the window seat, helping her stow her picnic bag first. When the bus started, they jostled together and she touched his leg with her knee. 'Excuse me,' she blushed. He waved a hand as if it were no matter, shifting the coat he held stiffly in his arms as they pulled out of the bus station.

'Nice day,' she tried, studying his secret face.

'No poison flowers of rain.'

'Pardon?'

His voice was foreign, but not foreign like Marguerite's, really foreign.

'My God, the rain,' he declared, loudly, 'and the dismal cold. It does not care how we come and go. I see nothing in this rain. I cannot paint when I cannot see. When there is no light, there is no hope.'

So he was the artistic type. 'Are you an oil painter, or a watercolorist?' He sounded like a poet. 'Your English is very good.'

'I am an exile.' He grimaced.

'Me too.'

'Here I am buried.' He gestured aggressively and kicked the floor of the bus as they drove passed a tar-macked railway platform and a breaker's yard. Beyond the outskirts of the Northern city, they found themselves in a still, mysteriously bleak landscape that could hook the unwary with its strange beauty.

'I'm from New York,' Marguerite said.

'New York is my dream.' He twisted towards her. 'A selfish amusement as I must return to Poland one day. My country has been crushed as a nation. Do you know why?'

Marguerite shook her head.

'The Soviet constitution chains the Polish people like chessboard prawns.'

'That stinks.'

'Only art will liberate Poland.'

'Art?'

'Of course.' He looked at her with frank appreciation, studying the curve of her shoulders, her plump arms, wide forehead, large breasts and full red lips. 'I know your name. It is *Woman*,' he said abruptly.

'No it's not. It's Marguerite.'

'Marek.' He held out his hand. His fingers were cold. 'Why are you here in Britain?'

'I'm a free spirit.' She didn't want to mention Colin.

'I do not meet a single other human being like you. You're very pretty,' he said. 'Beauty inspires me.'

She hadn't many defences. Her heart fluttered and her face lit up. 'This isn't a wedding ring.' She pulled at the gold band she wore. 'Don't think it's a wedding ring.'

'Weeding rings,' he scoffed. 'The institution of marriage means nothing to me.' Outside the window there was a sudden view of the sea. He reached for her hand. 'We are strangers together then,' he said. 'Maybe soulmates.'

The ruined castle was on a rise overlooking the North sea. The beaches they'd passed were still ringed in places with barbed wire. Concrete bunkers guarded the shore, although the war had been over for twelve years.

'The unforgiving sea,' Marek announced as they got out of the bus together. The air smelled sharply of salt. Gulls wheeled and cried overhead. 'I've brought a picnic.' Marguerite held up her string bag. 'C'mon share it with me?' As they passed along a bridge over a dry moat, through a gatehouse and into the castle grounds, she noticed no one but him. 'We share everything now,' he said meaningfully. But when they came to the turnstiles, he did not offer to pay her entrance fee. 'How can a moth pay?' He looked sorrowfully at her.

The castle was derelict, although the thick exterior walls and crenellated turrets were still standing. Inside a fortified enclosure, the remains of various domestic buildings described empty spaces labelled *Kitchen*, *Buttery*, or *Pantry*, on the open ground. Passing through them was like walking on top of a grassy floor plan. Marguerite's high heels sunk into the soft earth causing her to stumble. Marek took her arm.

Entering a ruined tower they looked up at a vault that resembled an opened umbrella. Walls, built to withstand siege, were pierced with slits through which longbows or crossbows could be fired. Marguerite removed her cardigan. She could smell a lilac bush on a warm breeze that dispersed the only remaining clouds, and turned the sky a flat, royal blue. She looked around amazed. 'This is heaven,' she said, as Marek found an isolated spot for them to sit and eat together.

'I bring this,' he removed a greasy package wrapped in newspaper from the pocket of his jacket. 'Polish sausage. Very spicy. Do you bring a knife?'

She shook her head. Her warm picnic bag lay between them. 'No mind.' He took a bite directly from the sausage and handed it to her. She took a bite. It was rich, dark and peppery like pastrami, only more so, with hints of bay and rosemary. 'Delicious.'

'My uncle's recipe. No seriously.' They passed the sausage back and forth. There was nothing to drink, no beer or wine. She couldn't afford drink. She fed him chicken and grapes from her fingers, but ate only a dainty little herself. Her appetite had gone. 'Delicious,' he tried to speak in her voice. She laughed in a carefree way, wiping her greasy hands on the grass. Ignoring a slight dampness, she lay on her back. 'In New York City we didn't have sky.' She was slightly dizzy. 'Or grass.'

'Come away with me?' he said suddenly, leaning over her.

'Where to,' she sat up, 'the dungeons?'

'Dungeons? I don't understand.'

'Where are we going then?'

'Italy, Spain, Portugal, Greece.'

'Are you serious?'

'We lay in the sun. I paint. You do something. We eat and drink. No, for you I will give up drinking. We make love.'

She blushed. 'You mean it?' She turned her head this way and that watching tourists in the distance wandering around the castle grounds.

'It comes to me like a picture. We can live in those places on air, sleeping on beaches, catching fish and picking fruit. You help me plan the liberation of Poland. Have you heard of Premier Gomulka?'

'We'll cut off his head!'

'No, no! He is a moderate. Not like Stalin.'

They both shuddered.

'Come with me Marguerite. You don't belong here in this tiny light. Here you reduce to a slim column.'

'I can't come.'

'You can.'

'I can't.'

'You must.'

'I'm so confused. Nothing like this has ever happened to me before,' she lied. In the past, she'd given up everything for unsuitable men, like her ex-boyfriend Ernie who was married to Selma. 'You're greedy for foolishness,' her mother had told her long ago.

Marek began to sketch Marguerite on the back of an envelope. 'American girl,' he called her, having briefly forgotten her name, 'turn this way.' Flattered, she held her head still, while a well of excitement bubbled up inside her. When he finished, he hid his work. 'I make a painting soon.' He tucked the envelope away. Tussling for it, she pushed him back against the grass and sank down on top of him. He wore tight trousers and a flowing white shirt. When he smiled, she could see he was missing some side teeth. Boldly she ran her hand along his body and felt his buttocks tighten. 'I don't have much, but I can promise you amusement,' he whispered, 'later when we are alone.'

She'd heard it all before, but it still excited her. He called her 'Venus.' She blushed like a sheltered girl. Captured without difficulty, she laid her head against his arm, lifted and kissed his hand. 'I penetrate your gate, I think, tonight.' He gave her a meaningful look. This was more than she'd ever hoped for from her day out. She refused to think about Colin.

Marek played with the ends of her hair, delighting her, then closed his eyes and fell asleep. She touched his cheek tenderly, but he didn't stir. 'Let's look at the keep,' she urged, shaking him.

'You go. I want to lie in the sun.'

'Please.' She got him to his feet. 'In these shoes I need you to hold me up.'

As they walked along together she was aware of people noticing them. What a couple we make, she thought proudly. When they climbed the stairs to the castle keep, she opened the large handbag she carried, took out a pair of flat shoes, and put them on. 'You tricked me,' he scolded with a laugh, 'later you will pay.' The chambers they entered lacked roofs and window glass. A lightwell, open to the sky, illuminated parts of the interior that would otherwise have been dark. 'An airshaft!' Marguerite cried. 'We had them in the Bronx.' Squeezing through a narrow passage, they arrived at a guardroom where a hole in the floor led to the dungeon. 'Like Poland,' Marek commented. They looked out a slender window towards a river and crouched together in an enormous fireplace. Their footsteps clanged like buckets. Using a rusty nail he found, Marek carved their first initials secretly in a corner of soot-blackened stone. M&M.

'I'll do it,' she whispered when she saw the silvery marks he'd made. 'I'll run away with you.'

'Do you promise?'

'I do. But you must take me as I am.' She was crazy. 'I cannot even bring a toothbrush. I have to leave my old life behind, as of now.' She dug in her pocket for her latchkey and tossed it over the castle wall.

'You're mine.' His eyes glittered.

Emerging, at last, into sunlight they blinked and strolled, arm in arm, down a grassy slope. On the lawn, in front of an underground passage, a tourist stood grasping two magnificent dogs on a lead. He looked very ordinary, surrounded by his family, but his dogs were devils with thick dark hair, heavy shoulders and proud heads. Marguerite hurried Marek towards them. But he resisted. 'Those types don't interest me,' he gestured, indicating the large loud family. 'Only we are the real ones.' He held her back with an iron grasp.

'But the dogs,' she said, breaking away. It made her feel ashamed of him. 'Beautiful dogs,' she told their owner as she approached the animals. Up close, the middle-aged man was small and stunted with a short neck. He wore a corduroy sports jacket, sandals and woolly socks. 'They're nervy,' he said. As one began to strain at the lead, the other barked. 'Give over,' he tried to settle them.

'There's something here they don't like,' an old lady at his side put in. The dogs whimpered. 'It's the crypt,' another, younger, woman beside her added, pushing the National Health glasses she wore up to the bridge of her nose, while the older lady nodded. 'Don't make a fuss,' the man told them. The children sat on a furrow in the ground. 'I'm fair beat,' one little girl complained.

From a distance, Marek watched them. Even though it was warm, he'd put on his coat and poked the collar up around his ears and throat.

'Do you think the crypt's haunted?' Marguerite asked.

'Are you American?' The man glanced at her, while Marek edged further away showing his dark, straight profile and the severe angle of his Slavic cheekbones. 'We don't see many Americans up here, do we Jean? We're from Shiremoor.' He pulled a big Northern handkerchief from his pocket and wiped his face. The younger of the two women shook her head.

Her hair was unattractively clipped. 'Do you believe in ghosts?' The dogs beat their tails.

'I'm not sure.'

'We're dowsers on the side.' She held up two shining metal rods. 'Usually we keep a shop. Do you want to have a go?' She beckoned Marguerite to the mouth of the crypt. 'England's full of ghosts.'

Marguerite looked over her shoulder at Marek. 'Come with me,' she called. But he shook his head, retreating even further from the group. 'Wait a minute,' she told the woman.

'You cannot go with them,' Marek said when Marguerite joined him.

'Why? It's great. They're great.'

'I'm asking you not to.' He showed his teeth.

'Don't be ridiculous, I'll just be a few minutes, if I survive,' she laughed.

'This is absolute. I forbid it.' His arms lifted and barred her way. Deciding he was only joking, she pushed past him. Then, turning around she opened her mouth and showed him the teasing point of her tongue.

Marguerite followed the dowsing woman underground into the dark mouth of the open, empty crypt.

'Not many come down here.'

A shaft of daylight lay across the dark stairs and dead air came out to meet them. Immediately she felt an oppressive damp. The walls were moist, reminding her of the bathroom in the flat she and Colin had rented in town. 'It's like nightime in here,' she said. There was gravel underfoot. The stones were green with moss. The only light came from windows lacking glass, set high up in the walls. The roof was vaulted, but it gave no feeling of space. Instinctively, Marguerite hunched her shoulders. The dowsing woman's glasses misted up.

'Hold one rod in each hand. Stick them straight out and walk slowly along that wall.'

Head bowed, Marguerite started to walk, clutching the carefully moulded handles of the rods. A rusty dampness crept through her shoes. Although she tried to hold them steady, the rods began to quiver and cross. She stopped dead. When she attempted to straighten them out, she found she could not. Her heart jumped inside her chest. On the gravel she saw a black knife for skinning, but when she stood over the spot, there was nothing but a dull stain on the ground.

From the shadows, the woman watched her closely. 'It's nasty,' she said knowingly. She closed her eyes and drew a quick breath. 'Someone has been bashed here.'

'Who?'

'Folks from olden days.'

Something about her mesmerised Marguerite. At first she'd appeared plain. Underground, she looked divine. 'I felt it.' Marguerite gazed in amazement at the slender gleaming rods.

'They crossed, did they? It's what they call psychic energy. The walls remember a heap of blather, badly off folk and dark business. Ganny twitched on every wall.'

'Ganny? I don't think we should be alone here.'

'Not me. I like this place. It's a canny miracle. The past has all been marked down here. Them rods is your eyes.' She patted Marguerite's hand. 'Why don't you have them, pet. Maybe you'll go dowsing again some day. I was very low meself before I found dowsing.' She looked meaningfully at Marguerite. 'A body could do worse.'

'They're yours. I couldn't take them.'

'Go on. They're just homemade. Nothing special. We bend them out of coathangers. Them handles are unscrewed bits a biro. Clever eh? We all have them. Even the children.'

'I thought maybe they belonged to Noah.'

'Whatever are you like?' the woman wondered.

Nodding, Marguerite put the rods under one arm. 'Must be midnight,' she laughed.

When she left the crypt, she searched for Marek. But he was no where in sight. The air felt velvety and dry. She stood for a moment breathing deeply, then walked back to where they had eaten their picnic. She couldn't wait to tell him what she'd experienced. However he wasn't in that place either. She looked over her shoulder. It was already four o'clock, time for the bus. Perhaps he was waiting there. She ran up to the door, but when she boarded, she saw his seat was empty and her lips went white. Panting down the aisle, she tried to get off again. 'Is there a problem?' the driver, a portly young man in a dark uniform, asked. 'This coach is about to depart.'

'You can't go,' Marguerite cried. She was taller than he was. 'We have to wait for Marek.'

'Marek?'

'The man who was sitting next to me.'

'A wee scabby fellow?' The driver winked at the other passengers as Marguerite peered over his shoulder. Her big front teeth caught the inside of her lower lip. She shifted the rods under her arm. 'Not at all.'

'He's done a flit has he?'

'I don't know what you mean.'

'Pardon Missus, but you were sitting alone.'

'What are you talking about? You think I'm dumb? There was a man next to me.'

'There wasn't.'

'He was a Polish artist.'

'Na, I didn't see him. I'm responsible for all the passengers on this trip. I'd have known. I do the tally. Marek?' he muttered, 'sounds like a character in a book.'

The others stared straight ahead. Miserably Marguerite brushed past their tweedy laps and found her seat. They stole him like thieves, she thought, looking at all their homely British faces. 'I don't even know his address,' she cried. She was still holding the dowsing rods she'd been given. They were only metal coathangers, which in itself was a marvel. She lay them gently across her lap.

Inside the bus, there was a tropical warmth A low afternoon sun turned the windows gold and dust motes floated in the air. When the engine started, after mis-firing a few times, and they swung slowly out of the parking area onto the main road, two women travelling together in the seat in front of Marguerite's linked arms and began singing '*The Isle of Capri*.' Both were poorly dressed. A man behind with a calm, smooth, careworn face, like Colin's, tapped her on the shoulder. She flinched away. But he only wanted to offer a packet of mints. 'Pass them along,' he said.

When the bus overheated and had to be parked at the side of the road with its bonnet up for the engine to cool down, the singing got louder. Helplessly, Marguerite joined in. She sang with the others until she became parched. Finally the tipsy old coach was re-started, belching black smoke. It was inevitable. Jolting, stuttering and weaving towards the town, Marguerite had to be carried home.